the BAD BOY bias

Tees&jeans

HALLIE BENNETT

Printed in the United States of America
Cover Design by The Arrowed Heart
ISBN: 978-1-955138-12-3
First Printing, 2021

BOOKS BY THIS AUTHOR

Standalones

Batter Up: An Instalove, Curvy Girl Romance

Wood Lessons: An Instalove, Curvy Girl Romance

Tees & Jeans Series

The Brother Bias: A Brother's Best Friend, Curvy Girl Romance

The Boss Bias: An Age Gap, Curvy Girl Romance

The Bad Boy Bias: An Opposites Attract, Curvy Girl Romance

Lumberjacks of High Ridge Series

Kept by the Beast: A Curvy Girl, Mountain Man Romance

Claimed by the Woodsman: A Surprise Pregnancy, Mountain Man Romance

Found by the Loner: A Curvy Girl, Mountain Man Romance

Curvy College Reunion Series

Campus Good Girl: A Curvy Girl/Jock Romance

Campus Queen: A Steamy Curvy Girl Romance

Campus Bookworm: A Shy Girl/Loner Guy Romance

Christmas & Curves Series

Festive Fever: A Curvy Girl Holiday Romance

PROLOGUE

FINN

Rock music attempts to drown out the buzzing of Kyle's tattoo machine as he works on his friend Michael. A man I cannot stand, but business is business. And since I own Valhalla Ink, one of the best local tattoo parlors around, making money is kind of a big fucking deal.

Adding more shading to the sketch I'm working on, I try to tune out the conversation the two are holding and focus on the woman coming to life in my notebook. Most of my drawings depict an aspect of Norse mythology due to my heritage, and this one's no different except the woman isn't some figment of my imagination. Instead, she bears a striking resemblance to a shy blonde who happens to be dating Michael. My grip tightens on the pencil, threatening to crack it at the reminder.

How a jackass like him managed to land such a sweet woman is beyond me—not to mention infuriating. The man doesn't deserve her; that's for damn sure.

And you do?

Probably not, but at least I'd treat her better than Michael. When he brought Abigail for the initial consultation for his current tattoo, Michael had spent the better part of the hour ignoring her while she sat ramrod straight—discomfort radiating from her curvy body. I tried bringing her into the conversation from my place on the sidelines but didn't have much luck. My efforts only elicited adorable blushes and stuttering responses.

Erasing a mistake on the curve of her cheek, I wonder where she is today as I fix the sketch. Curiosity getting the best of me, I casually ask, "How's Abigail? I'm surprised she's not here with you."

Michael scoffs. "I broke that off last week. The bitch is ice cold—wouldn't even let me touch her.

His offhand insult of Abigail rankles, but I can't deny a certain pleasure in hearing she refused the bastard's advances. "Seems like a *you* problem rather than hers. It's been my experience that if a man treats a woman right, then she's more than welcoming to his touch. And if he doesn't..." I let the sentence trail off and shrug—my meaning clear.

Kyle glances over at me, an eyebrow raised in question at the intentional baiting of his friend. Their friendship defies logic, with Kyle being a cool guy and Michael being an insufferable prick. But that's what childhood bonds will get you—stuck with someone out of sheer loyalty.

"You think you'd have better luck?" Michael's narrowed eyes take in my combat boots, the tattooed sleeves on my arms, and shaggy, shoulder-length hair with disbelief bordering on disgust. "You remember Abigail, right?"

Hell yeah. Plump ass, luscious tits, and a beautiful smile. How could I forget?

"Glasses, cardigan, card-carrying librarian? She sat quiet as a mouse when she was here, and you think you have a chance in hell that she'd let you touch her?" He snickers at the implausible scenario.

My molars grind together in annoyance because I know he's got a point. Women like Abigail don't frequent Valhalla Ink very often, and our brief encounter didn't bode well in my favor. An aura of quality emanates from her, a gentle reminder she's out of my league. "I didn't say that. She deserves better than either of us; just don't blame her for your own shortcomings."

"But you would rank yourself higher than me when it comes to getting in her pants." Like a dog with a bone, Michael persists in pushing me and throws out the final gauntlet. "I'd like to see you try. How about a wager? I bet you can't get one kiss from her, and if I'm right, you'll foot the bill for my next tat."

Kyle shakes his head while changing to a different needle. "Mike, come on..."

"What? It's just a friendly wager between men, so are you in?"

Closing my notebook, too distracted to continue working, I stand to my full six foot three height and sneer. "Wagers, bets? Games for boys. So, no, I'm not *in*."

"I knew you were all talk. Too scared to try because you know you'll lose."

I don't bother responding. Let him believe whatever the fuck he wants; it's no skin off my nose. Heading back to my office towards the rear of the shop, Michael's crowing follows me until the closing of the door shuts him out.

Jesus. A headache grows at my temples, and it's clear why. The man irks me; his only redeeming quality is that he introduced me to Abigail at his last appointment. Now even that possibility of seeing her again has disappeared.

Flipping open my sketchbook, various drawings of her fill the last twenty or so pages. I don't know why she has such a hold on me; an hour in a woman's presence shouldn't evoke such a visceral reaction of need. Yet, here I am—*fucking obsessed.*

A frustrated groan erupts as I toss the notebook aside, plopping into my desk chair before closing my eyes in a bid for peace. *Deep inhale, slow exhale.* Counting the breaths helps calm me, as does a picture of Abigail visiting the shop. Once my blood has cooled to a normal level, it's time to prepare for my next client and put the past twenty minutes out of mind.

Fuck Michael and his goading and his stupid bets.

CHAPTER ONE

FINN

ONE WEEK LATER

Hands propped on the steering wheel of my jeep, I wait for the light to change as my eyes catch on the building to the left of the intersection. The Smithfield Library. Abigail's probably in there right now, and an irresistible urge to see her causes me to hit the blinker to turn into the concrete lot and park.

Large windows covered in snowflakes and an orange fire blazing with the words "Warm up with a book" written across the glass span the front of the library. The clock on the dash reads five pm—an hour to closing. But I won't be here that long. Just a quick peek, then I'll go.

The knowledge of Michael and Abigail's break-up has weighed on my mind all week. She's free, and my dumbass thinks that means something. *Like you have a chance.* If I were smart, I'd shift back into drive and get the hell out of here instead of braving the bitter cold to enter the quiet library.

Two rows of computers separate the main portion of the library, and a couple of people sit spread out with blue light from the screens reflecting on their faces. Glancing towards the children's section on the right, I head in the opposite direction, hoping to find Abigail among the sea of bookshelves.

A layer of comfort falls on my shoulders at the scent of old books and the calm atmosphere. I don't spend a lot of time here, preferring to read on my phone when I have time, and the blunder of judgment kicks me in the gut. Abigail and I could've met months ago before she even knew Michael. *Which means she could've rejected you months ago, too, idiot.*

Sighing at the negative possibility, my pace slows as I nonchalantly stare down each aisle, trying to look like I belong and not desperately searching for the woman of my fantasies. Near the last row, I finally spot my quarry. Abigail pushes a cart full of books, her gaze studying the names and titles before placing them in their correct place on the shelf. Black boots cover her calves as dark jeans hug those generous hips and ass.

Damn, I could eat her up.

Like a stalker, I dip into the row behind her to follow her efficient movements—check, shelve, check, shelve. Thick, honey blonde waves swing just below her shoulders, shifting with each turn of her head. I'd like to catch those loose strands and tug her head back for a demanding kiss, but that's liable to get me thrown out of here and slapped with a restraining order.

Maybe later... when she's mine. If that ever happens.

My neck bends to peer between two shelves as we reach the end of the row, the awkward height emphasizing how ridiculous I must look. A grown man acting like a schoolboy spying on his crush. Huffing in scorn at the comparison, I immediately realize my mistake when Abigail freezes like a deer in headlights before twisting to face me.

"Hello?"

Embarrassed at being caught, I own up to my error and round the corner of the shelf between us with a stiff wave. "Hey... Abigail, right?" *As if I don't fucking know.*

Hazel eyes widen behind her glasses, and a scarlet hue spreads on her cheeks. "Uh, yeah... And you're Finn? You own Valhalla Ink. Did you need help to find a book?"

Irrational happiness that she remembers my name warms my gut. *More schoolboy shit.* "Just browsing for now. Unless there's something you'd recommend?"

"Well, we don't have the most up-to-date catalog, but I could probably find something you'd like. Are you sure you're in the right section, though?"

Suddenly, the small red hearts on all the book spines make sense as I understand what she means. Romance. Nothing wrong with a good love story, but it's not my usual reading material. A brief chuckle spills out at the realization as Abigail joins in with a humorous smile.

"I'm in the right section." *Because you're here.* "I'm ready to mix it up, so what do you suggest? What's your favorite?"

Tell me something, anything. I want to know everything about you.

"It's hard to narrow down to one, though you kind of remind me of characters from this motorcycle romance series I like..." She pauses, tugging on the sleeve of her cardigan before adjusting her glasses. "Sorry, I don't mean to stereotype." Her eyes tour over my body in apology, but I'm not offended. People assume certain things about me by the way I look and dress all the time.

"No worries; I'm not exactly a choir boy. Where's this book series? I think I'd like to check it out."

Abigail leads me to another aisle, her delicate rose scent providing the sweetest snare as I follow. One hand trails over the weathered book spines until she stops at the "C"s. A displeased sound rumbles from her throat, and the cute noise puts me in mind of a disgruntled kitten—making me want to pet and soothe. *Down, boy.*

"Problem?"

"The first book in the series is checked out already, and it's really best if you read these in order." Disappointment laces her tone as she taps the offending empty slot. Sighing, Abigail bites her lower lip, clearly trying to think of a solution while my thoughts have skipped past reading to tasting her mouth—the tender pink flesh calling to me.

"Why don't you let me know when it's available? You guys allow holds, right?" Her expression brightens, and I pat myself on the back for saving the moment. I may not frequent the library often, but I do understand the workings of their system.

"Of course! Let me grab your library card and get you sorted."

Once we've walked back to the front counter, she takes my card and starts typing into the computer. Silence falls except for the click clack of the keyboard—a perfect opportunity to gauge where her head's at concerning Michael. "I heard about your break-up. How are you doing?"

"Break-up makes the relationship sound like more than it was; we only went out on a few dates." Abigail slides my card across the linoleum countertop when she's finished. "And I understood his reasons for wanting to end things. To be honest, he kind of beat me to it, since it was obvious we weren't right for each other."

Truer words were never spoken, but can I be right for you?

"So, you're all good. No hard feelings."

"Pretty much." Her expression lightens with a professional smile, switching topics. "Now, you're all set for this hold, and the library will notify you when it comes in. Is there anything else I can help you with?" The abrupt change hits me in the face, and I feel the sting of her dismissal. *At least you got what you came here for.* For a last-minute decision, I managed to see and talk to her—more than I expected.

"No, thank you. I'm good for now, but I'll see you later? When I pick up the book?" The eager note in my voice can't be denied, but I hope she finds it endearing rather than desperate.

"If I'm working the counter. Otherwise, Amanda will assist you." She motions to an older woman checking in a load of books. The lady in question waves at the sound of her name, and it's obvious she's listened to our entire conversation by the inquisitive look in her rheumy eyes. "Thanks for stopping by. Have a good evening!"

I nod in farewell and retreat to my jeep. The lingering warmth of her presence sustains me as the winter chill nips at my skin before I settle in the raised seat—a plan forming in my mind. We'll meet again even if I have to troll the library until she's manning the counter. A possessive streak runs straight down from my head to my heart and even further to my semi-hard cock.

She's out of my league, but I want her.

Abigail's going to be mine.

CHAPTER TWO

ABIGAIL

Amanda scoots closer after Finn leaves, excitement radiating from her frail body. "Who was that hunk of man candy?"

Laughing at the apt description, I try to appear unaffected by Finn's visit. With long hair and tats covering his body, his resemblance to Charlie Hunnam from Sons of Anarchy is undeniable and sexy. Which is why my first thought when he'd asked for a book was to recommend a motorcycle club romance—an entire smorgasbord of dangerous bikers in leather. Not that I've seen Finn riding a motorcycle, but it wouldn't surprise me if he owned one.

"Just a patron searching for something to read," I toss out like it doesn't matter to me one way or the other. Even though his shocking arrival and our subsequent conversation had set off an explosion of nerves, heat, and confusion—a volatile mix in my usually calm body.

"Seemed like more than that with the way he eye-fucked you the whole time."

"Amanda!" I gasp and shush her with a pleading wave, my gaze furiously scanning the vicinity to see if anyone else heard her. "There are children here! Besides, I think you misinterpreted whatever you saw; he wasn't... well, you know. He's not interested in me. We've only met once."

"Once was all it took for me and Jimmy," she warns before toddering off to start our closing routine for the day. Unwillingly, I stare at the parking lot as if Finn's still outside— waiting for me—and the absurd thought brings me back to reality.

A man like that? Danger wrapped in seductive ink and muscles. Something that doesn't pair well with knit sweaters and a virgin in every way—no tattoos or piercings and no men ever. Hell, I couldn't even watch Sons of Anarchy because of the violence. Yet I think I can handle a man who looks like he'd fit right into that world?

Not that I've had much luck with other types of guys...

My fleeting interlude with Michael was a mistake, an attempt to fix the whole virgin problem, but in the end, I couldn't even let him touch me. After nearly thirty years of being alone with little physical contact with others, the idea of breaking that record with him just hadn't felt right.

My family were never huggers or prone to discussing feelings and that 'hands off' vibe has followed me through life. It took me years before getting used to my best friends', Ella and Saoirse's, touch—the impromptu hugs or random playful bumps. Is it any wonder I couldn't bear a kiss from Michael?

Honestly, I'm not sure what prompted him to ask me out when he visited the library a month ago. But since he was the only man to ever show interest in me—and my thirtieth birthday was right around the corner—I figured, what could it hurt?

The lights above flash to signal fifteen minutes until closing and serve as my cue to stop thinking about Finn. He stopped by the library like every other Smithfield resident. So, what? It doesn't mean he's into me or that I should consider whether to let him touch me or not.

Best to stick with what I know. For almost thirty years, I've been single because no man has seriously approached me with interest—Michael was a weird fluke. And I don't foresee that changing anytime soon.

STEPPING INSIDE MY apartment, I hang my purse and coat on hooks by the door. My shoes are barely kicked off when someone knocks with a rapid rhythm. "Hang on," I call, hopping over to the door to let Ella and Saoirse in. They want to talk about my birthday, although it's going to be a quiet night in town.

"Hey, are we too early?" Ella spies my haphazardly thrown shoes against the welcome bench I have set up as part of a makeshift mudroom area.

"No, it's fine. You guys get settled while I change into something comfier." After meeting in college, we liked to call ourselves the Tees & Jeans Club because we stuck to casual t-shirts and jeans, promising to always stay true to those down-to-earth roots. Our wardrobes have changed over the years, but the sentiment remains—at our cores we're still those girls from college.

Clad in an oversized tee and sleep shorts, I return to the living room where a box of pizza sits on my coffee table. My stomach growls before I pluck two slices of pepperoni from the box and curl up on the couch.

"Okay, so we've been talking," Saoirse starts with a no-nonsense expression. "You'll be thirty next week, and we're determined to help you break out of this bubble you've formed around yourself. Help you take some risks." As the most outgoing of us, it's no surprise Saoirse's the one to broach this subject.

"What about Michael? Dating a man was a pretty big step for me."

"And we approve of the effort, if not the man." Ella's nose wrinkles in displeasure. Probably remembering the dreadful group date we went on. Michael didn't get along with Gavin or Thomas—Ella and Abigail's significant others—and he'd monopolized the conversation the entire night.

The more I think back on the time spent with Michael, the more I cringe. *Desperation leads to questionable decisions...and a lowering of standards.*

"Agreed. We'll keep working on the relationship front, though I'm not sure how we can help with the touching issue." Saoirse's green eyes soften at the mention of my biggest hurdle to overcome. It's grown into this three-horned beast, despite my best efforts. And a secret part of me believes it'll only go away with the right man, like I live in a romance novel instead of this small town. That somehow my body will recognize its mate and learn to relax.

"One step at a time," Ella promises. "But there's more to life than men. We're thinking of getting tattoos to celebrate our little club."

"I thought that's what the photoshoot is for—to commemorate ten years." Next month, we have an appointment with a professional photographer to take shots of us in our classic white tees and blue jeans attire in honor of a friendship continuing to stay strong after a decade.

"We're still doing that, but tattoos could be fun, too. It'll up our sexy factor." Saoirse's eyebrows raise suggestively, and I shake my head at the notion.

"You're already sexy, and I don't like pain. But if the two of you are looking for a place to get them, I know a reputable tattoo parlor." A picture of Finn materializes, and I duck my head to avoid having them see the heat suffuse my cheeks. *No such luck.*

"Oh, really?"

"Yes, do tell. How do you know about tattoo parlors?"

Licking dry lips, I tear the last bit of pizza crust on my plate, building a mountain of crumbs as I consider the question. "Michael took me to one weeks ago. It's called Valhalla Ink, and the owner, Finn, was really nice, and he showed up at the library tonight." The words rush out towards the end. Telling them about our run-in tonight wasn't part of my plan, but it slipped out—needing to be voiced.

"We've been here for how long, and you're just now telling us you had a man visit you at work?"

"He didn't visit me specifically. He was looking for a book, and I happened to be the librarian he found. Except I couldn't help him because what I suggested was already checked out, so we had to put it on hold for when it gets returned." Maybe I should've gone with a backup suggestion. The thought hadn't occurred to me at the time; I'd been too flustered to think straight with Finn's heat and clean, male scent enveloping me.

"Oh, why don't you drop it off at his tattoo parlor when it comes in?" Saoirse suggests, readjusting her position in the armchair to my right.

"Why? I'll possibly see him when he picks the book up."

"And you'll be working, which doesn't leave much time for talking. If you deliver the book to him, it'll be the perfect opportunity to chat, and he'll see how interested you are." Ella and Saoirse exchange excited grins as their hair-brained scheme takes shape.

"Who said I was?"

"The blushing doesn't lie. But even if you weren't, it's another man to learn to get comfortable around. That'll be a win in and of itself."

"Maybe..." The idea of walking into Valhalla Ink alone on the premise of giving Finn a book scares and intrigues me. It's out of my comfort zone, but they have a point. My life needs a good shake. This could be a healthy baby step.

Plus, I secretly made a vow on my last birthday that I'd have my first kiss before turning thirty, and time's almost up. Things didn't work out with Michael, and I doubt Finn is the man for me. But at least I'll be able to say I tried because it's more than I've been able to say for the past twenty-nine years.

CHAPTER THREE

FINN

The bell above the shop door rings, signaling another customer, and I call out, "Just a minute." With a last swipe of the rag and disinfectant, my work area is clean again and ready for my next appointment.

"No need to rush; I'm just dropping this off for you." The dulcet tones of Abigail send a shock wave through my body. Her unexpected arrival has all sorts of questions flying around in my head, but whatever the reason, I'm glad to see her again so soon.

"Hey! What's up?"

She brandishes a dark book before offering it to me. "Your hold came in, and I thought I'd save you a trip to the library—small town hospitality and all that." Her hazel eyes avoid mine as she focuses on the open binder of tattoo designs on the counter, a pink-tipped finger tracing a drawing of a butterfly.

"Thanks for this; I appreciate it." Taking the book, I glance at the cover of the back of a man as he rides off on a motorcycle before tucking it behind the counter. She didn't have to make this trip, yet she did. That has to mean something, right? Optimism sprouts in my heart at the possibility.

Abigail's attention remains on the tattoos, and I ask, "Are you interested in getting something for yourself?"

All I see is smooth skin—a perfect canvas for me—and I'd bet she's a tattoo virgin. *No doubt she's a virgin in every way if touching is an issue for her.*

"Oh, no, I don't think I'd handle it very well.. Pain and I aren't good friends. I don't even have my ears pierced." She pushes a wave of hair back to reveal earlobes free of piercings. My teeth ache to nibble on the delicate flesh, but I quickly reign in the urge.

"Not a problem. I could give you a temporary one."

"Like a peel and stick? I'm surprised you'd offer those here."

"We get all kinds of customers, and you're not the first one to express worry over pain. But I was thinking of something a little different. I could draw the design with special markers meant for skin—almost like henna but not quite." My mind races with ideas: a floral bracelet to suit her preference for rose perfume or books with a favorite quote of hers. *Or my name to lay claim to her.*

Time stretches between us as I wait for her decision, and I wonder if there's anything else I can say to sway her to my side. Promise to be careful. To abide by her boundaries.

"When would we do it? I'm on my lunch break now, and I'm sure you have a full day scheduled already."

Victory. "How about tomorrow during your break? And if you don't have a preference, I can come up with a design for you." *Make everything as easy as possible, so she doesn't change her mind.*

"Alright, tomorrow. I'll see you then." Abigail gives a short wave of farewell before leaving, and an irrepressible smile forms at the knowledge that I'm going to see her again.

"Was that Abigail?" Kyle comes up behind me after finishing with a client. "What's she doing here?"

"She's interested in a temporary tattoo." I skip mentioning the book; Kyle doesn't need to know everything.

"How's that going to work with her touching problem? Man, Mike's going to have a field day with this."

He chuckles while typing in information on the front work computer, and my gut tightens in annoyance. "You're not going to tell him. What Abigail does isn't his business anymore." *And never will be again if I have my way.*

Kyle's forehead scrunches in confusion. "You're not thinking of going there, are you? Michael can be an ass sometimes, but he made a good point last time. I'm not sure you're her type."

"Let me worry about Abigail." I don't need his doubts fueling my own. She fucking came to me today. *Me.* The shaggy-haired and tattooed parlor owner. I can work with that first step given a little time.

Loath to continue this line of questioning, I brusquely check with him about the rest of the day's appointments—the subtext reading that our previous discussion is over.

CHAPTER FOUR

ABIGAIL

What am I doing?

When Finn offered to give me a temporary tattoo, my initial instinct had been to say "No". Not due to lack of interest but out of fear. Which is what pushed me to agree and come back today.

Ella, Saoirse, and I can talk about ways to step out of my comfort zone, but it's up to me to actually accept opportunities—to make that first step. Hopefully, I don't regret this particular one. Anxiety causes sweat to form on my overheated skin, and my heart's pumping a mile a minute. Logic tries reminding me not to blow this out of proportion; it's supposed to be a fun adventure, getting a tattoo. However, reason doesn't hold a candle to the sweeping worry pervading my body.

Is it too late to back out?

Yes.

My car's parked, and I'm wasting time sitting here overthinking versus going inside and proving it's no big deal. Taking a deep breath, I shore up my courage, grab my purse, and get out. A couple of other vehicles are in the lot as well, and it occurs to me that there could be an audience for our session. The possibility almost makes me turn around.

Multiple pairs of eyes greet me as I enter the cool interior of the parlor. Waiting clients stare—a menagerie of people covered in ink. Clearly, I don't belong here.

"Abigail, I'm glad you made it. Follow me." Finn appears like magic, and I appreciate his presence. At least, I won't have to sit awkwardly waiting up front with everyone else.

"Are you sure it's a good time? You look pretty busy."

"Those are Kyle and Mandy's clients; I don't think you've met her yet." He holds a hand out to motion me inside a square space with two chairs. Light-colored walls stand slightly higher than my waist to provide a semblance of privacy. "So, there's no need to worry. You're my priority—no one else."

The bold statement sounds more proprietary than I'm sure he means it to be, but a shiver of excitement shoots through me nonetheless, converting part of my nervous energy into something more pleasurable. Sitting in the larger chair, I scoot until my back hits the leather. My ankles cross, hands resting in my lap, while Finn shows me a pretty design of an open book with flowers blooming from the center.

"Oh, that's beautiful! Can you put it on my wrist? Or the back of my hand? Somewhere easy and manageable." Thankfully, the library doesn't have strict rules about tattoos, so I won't have to hide his art which obviously is meant for display.

His talent surprises me. When I think of artists, I picture a more sensitive type painting detailed canvases. The delicate work Finn created proves my preconceived notions need to be adjusted.

"Great minds think alike." He washes his hands before putting on gloves and dropping into a rolling chair next to mine, wheeling closer. Pulling over a silver tray and a cushioned armrest, Finn lifts a set of markers. "Just so you know, these are brand new, never been used before, for your protection. Lay your arm over this—wrist up—and we'll get started, so you're not late returning to work."

Work. The library.

For a moment, real life had retreated like Valhalla Ink truly was a door to another world. Various drawings adorned the walls of the parlor, but an obvious Norse theme pulled it all together. Ever since I met Finn, his Sons of Anarchy vibes have dominated my mind, but I can see a bit of Thor in there, too.

A Viking image of him ravaging my body pulses in my core, and mortification floods my system. *You can't think like that when the man's literally right in front of you!*

Oblivious to my inappropriate thoughts, Finn lifts a hand up, pausing before beginning. "I've got to hold your arm steady with one hand while I draw with the other. Is that okay?"

The kind gesture wrings a swell of emotion from my chest. No one ever asks before touching, never checks my boundaries. But this man did—with no prompting and against any expectations. Then it occurs to me why he might pose the question.

"Michael said something, didn't he?" Humiliation leaves me frozen as I read the truth in his sympathetic gaze.

"Just in passing. I overheard a conversation between him and Kyle. But it's not a problem; whatever you're comfortable with works for me." *It didn't for Michael.* My resistance to his touch was the largest issue between us.

"You can do what you need to." I nod for him to get started, and he grins like my acceptance made him proud. The first cold brush of the ink-tipped marker tickles, but it's his warm hand on my forearm that draws my attention. A layer of latex separates us—a thin barrier that does nothing to diminish Finn's heat.

Attempting to focus elsewhere, I explain, "Professional touches don't bother me as much as... personal ones." An awkward laugh bubbles up. "Honestly, there isn't an excellent reason for the aversion except for years of touch-deprivation that have built into this mountain which seems too high to surmount."

Despite my embarrassment, it's nice sharing with him. Maybe because he's practically a stranger, or maybe it's the unusual connection I feel with him. Either way, I ramble, trying to help him understand while he calmly listens.

The glide of the marker is soothing as the design comes to life. Mesmerizing and impressive. It's obvious why Finn is so sought after. Before Michael brought me to Valhalla Ink, I'd looked up reviews online, and most of them sang Finn's praises.

"Scaling a mountain doesn't happen overnight; it takes patience and time. Don't beat yourself up about it." His thumb caresses my skin, almost absent-mindedly, but the repetitive motion comforts me. Once again, he upends my expectations with sweet understanding. "Besides, a man worth his salt will know you're worth waiting for."

My heart stutters as Finn glances up at me, his mouth hovering above my wrist before blowing a soft, warm breath across the drying ink. Thighs clenching instinctively, the intimate action lights me up like a firework in the night sky. Michael never caused such a reaction, and it confirms I made the right decision. Not settling or giving into his wants before I was ready.

Another smile forms on his bearded face, and he changes the subject. "So, does anyone ever call you 'Abby'?" A pink rose blooms above the book he's drawn, and the vibrant colors almost make me wish it was permanent.

"Not really. I wouldn't have an issue with it if they did, but I think there's something about me that gives off more of an Abigail vibe. Old-fashioned, closed-off? Like people aren't comfortable with the familiarity of Abby." Although Ella and Saoirse used to call me by the shortened version of my name after we first met, it quickly dwindled until they stuck with plain 'Abigail'. I never asked about the change since it wasn't a big deal, but maybe I should have questioned it.

"Abigail's a pretty name. Old-fashioned maybe, but not closed-off. And neither are you. If it's alright, you can be Abby to me."

"I'd like that." It feels special—having a nickname only he uses. Curiosity blooms as I imagine what being special to Finn means and wonder why it matters so much to me.

Isn't it obvious?

You've never been special to a man in your life. Isn't it about time you found out what it's like? Finn smiles at my acceptance before continuing to draw. I study his intent expression and make my decision.

Yes, it's about damn time I discover what it's like to belong to a man—to belong to this man. *If only he'll have me...*

CHAPTER FIVE

FINN

A few days after finishing Abby's temporary tattoo, I finish the book she gave me and debate my next move. Return it to the library like a normal citizen—dropping it off in the return slot? Or go out on a limb and deliver it in person?

Our last conversation flowed easily once we got past the difficult parts about her touching issue, and the insight into her personal life made me hungry for more. It'd even pushed me to be bold enough to ask if it'd be okay to keep in contact, exchanging phone numbers to message each other.

"Hey, would it be possible for me to see you tonight? I'd like to drop off the book but won't be free until after the library closes..." My plan is full of holes, but I hope she doesn't question it. Tomorrow is as good a day as any to bring the book back, but I want to see her tonight. Maybe I'll get lucky, and she'll agree.

"Why don't you come by after you're done? I'm closing alone tonight, so you can keep me company."

Fuck yeah!

"Sounds like a plan. I'll even bring dinner. Any particular favorite?"

"Surprise me." *Will do, baby.*

HOURS LATER, NIGHT has fallen, and I knock on the library door, hands full of food and drinks. My breath puffs out in bursts of heat, disrupting the wintry air, before Abby hurries forward to let me in. "Come in, come in. It's freezing out here."

Clad in her usual jeans and a cozy sweater, warmth and comfort emanate from her, and I want to bask in the warm glow. "No kidding... How was work today?"

She leads me to an empty study table where I set our dinner down. "Oh, you know, another exciting day in the life of a librarian. A new shipment of books arrived, so we had fun cataloging those. How about you?"

Doling out burgers, fries, and drinks, we each take a seat and dig in as I share how my day went. The domestic scene of sharing our days acts as a catharsis from the concern I had earlier about overstepping a boundary by asking to see her in-person after work. I could get used to evenings spent like this—together and content.

A phone interrupts our conversation, and Abby jumps to answer it, hopping up on the counter to reach over for the receiver. When the call ends after a few minutes, I ask, "I'm surprised someone's calling after hours."

"It's not as unusual as you'd think. Most people don't look up our hours, so a lot of the calls are checking to see if we're still open. I've mentioned to our board that it'd be helpful to add an automated system for these calls, but it's not in our budget."

"That sucks because it seems like it'd be a good investment." But I understand money being tight, and unfortunately, public services like the library usually get the short end of the stick when it comes to funding.

"It is what it is." Abby's leg swings back and forth from her perch on the counter, her back resting against the wall as she tosses the empty burger wrapper in the trash. "Kobe!" The balled-up paper lands in the basket, and I laugh.

"Kobe? You a basketball fan?"

"Not really. It's actually my least favorite sport." Her nose wrinkles in dislike. And my heart skips at the adorable expression. *Fuck, I've got it bad.* "But in college, the guys always used to yell Kobe's name after shooting their shot. I guess it rubbed off on me."

Straightening from my seat at the table, I walk closer to stand in front of her. Curious eyes track the movement—thankfully, *only* curiosity, no fear. And I shoot my own shot. "I like the idea of rubbing off on you."

"Really?" The low timber of her query caresses my nerve endings as I inch nearer.

"Baby, I'd like to do a hell of a lot more if you'd let me." Carefully, my hands brace against the wall on either side of her, and I lean forward until a sliver of space remains between us. "If I promise not to touch, will you let me tell you what I'd like to do to this curvy little body?"

"Yes." The breathy word comes out quiet but firm, and desire burns in my blood. Swallowing hard, fantasies abound—making it hard to pick one to share.

"We've just gotten home after a night strolling down Main Street, enjoying ice cream sundaes from Fran's." One of the most popular local restaurants in town, Fran's is known for its slow-churned custard. "All evening I've wanted to corner you in some dark alley or doorway, to taste the sugar on your lips, but you insisted on waiting until we were home. Because you're a good girl. The sweet, little librarian who can't get caught in public with her man's mouth exploring every inch of exposed skin he can get to."

Abby's chest expands in a quick inhale of shock, but she doesn't ask me to stop. "Now, we are alone, and I can do whatever I want with you, Abby-mine. Like licking along the dimple on your right cheek before devouring the vanilla cream from your lips. You taste so sweet, baby."

She wets her lips as if experiencing it herself, and my eyes watch the movement, wishing it was my tongue swiping over her pretty bow mouth. Talking about kissing her makes my cock swell against my jeans' zipper, and I fear coming in my pants like a teenager before we're done tonight.

"What happens next?" she asks, a husky note entering her voice.

So far, so good.

"You open up for me, and I take your mouth like my cock will take your pussy. Hard and savage. Forcing you to submit and accept that your man's going to fuck you long and hard."

A shudder runs through her as a moan reaches my ears. Abby's definitely into this, and I'm determined to bring her to orgasm if it's the last thing I do. I've never made a woman come with words alone, but a challenge has never fazed me before.

"My hands skim over your belly until I cup your tits—soft, round, and ready to be suckled, aren't they?" Abby arches her back, and I wish her sweater wasn't so thick because there's no doubt in my mind that her nipples are swollen and aching behind the woolen fabric.

"I strip you down to nothing—bare to me, trembling in need. Your legs widen, beckoning my touch, and you know I can't let my girl down. My fingers sift through your curls until I reach your wet center. So slick. So hot. What gets you off, baby? Circles around your clit? Should I milk your little button while I suck your tit? Would you like that?"

Her hips jerk like my hand really is between her thighs, and a telltale quiver shakes her body with the force of her orgasm. I'm not far behind as cum soaks the front of my jeans—from the fantasy, from her visible pleasure. Our harsh breathing mingles in the quiet library, and fuck am I ready for more. The most explosive, intimate moment of my life, and we haven't even touched yet.

This woman has me spellbound by sensual magic, and I don't even think she realizes the power she holds.

"That was... something else."

"It was fucking incredible," I correct, chest heaving with deep gulps of air.

"Yeah, incredible," she repeats, amazement shining through her eyes, along with another emotion I can't quite pinpoint. But one thing's sure as hell: I wouldn't mind seeing this look for the rest of my life.

CHAPTER SIX

ABIGAIL

O*h my god.*

My hands grip the edge of the counter I'm sitting on, the hard edge digging into my skin. A pleasant warmth tingles along my nerve endings after my mini orgasm. An orgasm where Finn kept his hands to himself, but his words... *Wow.* The man has a dirty mouth, and I want to know what else it can do.

Fear of a man's touch—of allowing the wrong man that privilege—evaporates in the wake of what just happened. Finn's blown all of it out of the water and in the nick of time. Tomorrow marks my birthday, and I'm determined to cross "Have my first kiss before 30" off the list.

"Finn... Kiss me, please."

He jerks back in surprise at the request. "What? Abby, don't feel like I expect you..."

Shaking my head in denial, I place a hesitant hand on his shoulder—the first point of contact we've had tonight. "I know. You've respected all of my boundaries, and I'm telling you I want my first kiss to be with you. Now. Are you going to make me beg?"

His eyes darken before dropping to my mouth. "Not yet, baby."

Relief courses down my spine along with anticipation. Finn's going to kiss me. *Finally.*

Angling forward, his long hair forms a curtain around our faces. The scratch of his beard grazes my cheeks before seeking lips find mine. A mutual sound of gratification vibrates between us as our mouths meet in a clash of teeth and tongues—rough and ravishing, just like he'd promised.

All this time nerves and anxiety have plagued my thoughts about letting a man touch me, about not knowing what to do or how to handle it. But none of that matters now. Finn's desire heightens my own, and those are the only emotions that belong in this moment.

Strong hands tangle in my hair and tilt my head to the side as he deepens the kiss. My glasses press into the bridge of my nose, but I ignore the discomfort. The aggressive rasp of Finn's tongue along mine draws all of my attention. It feels like a possessive claim which is something I want more than anything, and a decision solidifies in my mind. *Can I really do this?* Pulling back, words burst from me before I chicken out. "Will you take me home tonight? Make love to me?"

"You're determined to kill me, aren't you?" A brief, incredulous chuckle rumbles from his chest. "There's nothing I'd love more, baby, but is it what you really want? Emotions are riding high, and I don't want you to regret anything."

His concern does the opposite of his intention—proving this is the right decision versus making me reconsider. Finn cares about my welfare. This is more than a quick hook-up for him. Otherwise, why put me off? If this were Michael, we wouldn't even be debating the subject. I'm sure he would've had me carted out to the parking lot by this point.

"It may seem rash, but my birthday starts at midnight. I want to be with you, in your arms. It's the only gift I want."

He paces away, and I immediately miss his heat while awaiting the verdict.

"Midnight?" Brown eyes glance back at me, and I nod in confirmation. "Then, we have a few hours. We'll both go home, and you'll have time to think about whether this is a step you're prepared to make. If you don't change your mind, I'll be waiting for you at my place. But I warn you: at midnight, if you decide to give yourself to me, that's it. That shit means forever, Abby-mine, because once I have you, I'm not letting go."

That's the idea.

My whole life I've clung to romantic dreams—read happily-ever-afters. I want my own with Finn. There's always been a part of me that's known it was only ever going to be one man for me, however silly it seemed. But my heart was right to wait. Now it's time for my reward—in the form of a tall, tattooed man who looks like he can rescue me from hell before bringing me to heaven.

"Deal." Vaulting off the counter, I stumble in my eagerness before Finn catches me. "Text me your address, and I'll be there like Cinderella... Though, this is opposite of that, but you understand." Anticipation sends me into rambling, flustered by all the possibilities of tonight.

This is gonna be one hell of a birthday.

CHAPTER SEVEN

FINN

Once we decided on a course of action, Abby hurried to complete the rest of her library closing duties, and I waited to see her safely to her car. My head's reeling from tonight's revelations, and the night's still young.

What started like any other day has quickly escalated into one of the best days of my life. Somehow, I breached Abby's guarded heart and broke through her fear of touch. *Damn, my girl's strong and brave.* She trusts me enough to give herself to me. To set aside her anxiety and let me love her. I can't fucking believe it, but I won't waste this opportunity.

If she shows up. She might come to her senses first.

Ignoring the pessimistic thought, my first stop after leaving the library is the one big box store Smithfield has to pick up supplies. Abby might not come, but if she does, I'll be ready. She won't regret placing herself in my hands and becoming mine.

Trolling the aisles for food and anything else to make my place more romantic, the trip takes about fifteen minutes before I'm headed home, prepared for the evening. *Hopefully.*

My two bedroom home sits at the end of the street, toeing the line between town and unincorporated land. Hustling inside, I tidy the comfortable space and start setting up for Abby's arrival. Once the tasks are completed, a shower calls my name and offers a way to kill some time while I wait. Everything seems to move in slow-motion, increasing my trepidation.

What if she changes her mind?

An alarm rings on my phone hours later, signaling the time. Midnight. On cue, a light knock raps on the front door, and disbelief mingles with joy. Abby came.

Whipping the door open, I motion her inside with a grin. "You're here."

"Told you I would be." Her hair's a little damp from her own shower, and the signature rose scent rises stronger than ever. Thigh high socks peek above tall boots, and the sliver of skin exposed between the socks and her short sweater dress is temptation incarnate.

"I know it's late, but I bought some champagne and dessert to celebrate your birthday." Leading her to the living room, where a blaze burns in the fireplace, my earlier efforts are revealed. Doubt tries to cast a shadow until a delighted gasp bubbles up from Abby as a hand covers her heart.

"You did this? For me?" Happiness shines from her eyes, and pride swells in my chest. Yeah, this was definitely the right call.

Heaps of blankets and pillows lie in front of the fire, creating a cozy nest while clear Christmas lights add a soft border around the area. Thankfully, the store still had leftover lights from the holidays, and I grabbed all of them. I've never made something like this before, but I want Abby's first time to be special—want our first time together to be as perfect as possible.

"It's not too much? The bed might be more comfortable, but I thought..."

"No, this is perfect. Thank you... I never would've expected something like this from—" Her sentence cuts off as she realizes how it might sound, and an apologetic look enters her eyes.

"A guy like me?" I shrug, unoffended by the assumption. "To be honest, you're the first person I've ever done something like this for. You deserve to be romanced and worshiped."

Squeezing my arm in appreciation, a sheen of tears glimmers in Abby's gaze. "No one's ever said or done anything like this for me. I actually gave up hope it would ever happen..." The sentence fades, and her head dips in shyness.

"Get ready, baby, because I'm going to give you everything." I can't resist pulling her closer for a kiss of promise, not wanting her to hide from me. Intending to alleviate any fears, I dive into the deep end. "So, what'll it be? Food or sex?"

A watery laugh erupts as she considers the question. "Working up an appetite could be fun." One of her hands hesitantly trails down my chest and stomach.

Damn right. It'll be the most fun.

"Good choice. Though, I'm partial to dessert... Maybe just a teaser?" I guide her down into the nest of blankets and begin removing her boots. "These can stay for now." I smooth my hands over the thigh highs encasing her sexy as fuck legs. Sliding under the skirt of her dress, I drag the heavy fabric over her body as she wiggles her curvy body to hurry the process. Pale skin gleams in the flickering light after the last of her clothing disappeared, and an eager growl of need purrs in my throat. "One of these days, I want to draw you like this. Vulnerable and voluptuous. That can be the name of the series."

She laughs then teases. "So, you're going to paint me like one of your French girls?" The Titanic reference isn't lost on me, but I couldn't care less about other women.

"No, I'm going to paint you like you're *my* girl."

Her mouth forms a soft "Oh" of surprise, and I smile at the sight. Licking two of my fingertips, I draw a wet line down the center of her chest, sweeping under the curve of her tits before tracing a turgid nipple.

Firelight plays over Abby's face, and the importance of this moment weighs on my heart. I want to make her feel good—want to satisfy her every need. Like a fragile treasure in my palm, the need to protect and hoard for myself runs wild.

"Remember what I said about dessert? You ready to feed me, Abby-mine?" My fingers dip lower to gather the dew between her plump folds. Bringing glossy fingertips to my mouth, I suck them clean, immediately addicted to the spicy sweet flavor.

I fucking need more.

A keening cry of assent flutters from her lips before I brush a kiss over her exposed thigh. Licking along a delicate blue vein, I burrow deeper between her legs, darkness encapsulating me along with the scent of her arousal.

Mouth watering, my thumbs spread dark blonde curls while my nose nudges her clit, wetness coating the tip. "You're already soaked, baby, and we haven't even started yet. This pretty pussy's desperate for attention, isn't it?"

A pleading hum vibrates through her body as her hips hitch higher, encouraging me to continue. Not one to disappoint, I nibble along her sensitive folds and moan at the intoxicating taste. Sweetest pussy I've ever eaten—that's for damn sure.

But that's no surprise. Abby had me wrapped around her finger from the moment I first saw her at Valhalla Ink. She's my dream girl come to life—kind and smart, with gorgeous curves meant for my hands and mouth. Tonight may only be a one-time deal, but I'm going to do everything in my power to ensure it's not. That she comes back to me. Needs *me*.

Which starts with making her come at least a half dozen times—satisfy her so well she's too exhausted to leave tomorrow. Maybe that should be my plan. Make it impossible for her to physically leave me because she's too tired and sore from fucking.

My tongue plunges into Abby's quivering pussy, the walls tightening to hold me in place, but I retreat before flicking her engorged clit. "You're so tight, baby. I need to make sure you're soft and slick—able to accept my cock without pain." I press two fingers to her opening, stroking deeper to rub against her g-spot. "Because my cock's thick, Abby-mine, not gonna lie. But I'll make sure we fit."

"I know you will..." Abby breathes out; her confidence and trust warming me.

Wet, sucking sounds emanate from my thrusting fingers, and I wrap eager lips around her clit, drawing hard on the bundle of nerves, knowing she's close to climax.

Give it to me. I want to hear you come.

A piercing cry rents the air before she spasms in pleasure, a rush of hot cream hitting my tongue—the taste richer, more decadent.

Fucking delicious.

"You taste so good, baby. I could eat you all night long." And I would if my swollen dick wasn't ready to blow at any moment.

Another time.

CHAPTER EIGHT

ABIGAIL

Finn's mouth covers my sex, continuing his ministrations as my orgasm slowly subsides. Reaching a hand down, I cup the back of his head. In gratitude? For more? I'm not sure. All that's clear is that I need to hold a part of him. My heart and soul need that connection after withholding it for so long.

Gradually, he eases away from my sensitive center to pepper light kisses over my thighs before raising himself above me, his face thrown in shadow. "How are you doing? Still with me?"

"Yes, very much so," I confirm, basking in the glow of firelight and post-coital bliss. What a glorious way to begin my birthday, and he's still dressed! I can't imagine what having his naked skin sliding against mine will feel like—all those tattoos free for me to explore. And to have him fill me like no one ever has before... A shiver of anticipation travels down my spine. I don't want to wait any longer.

Finn holds his large body over mine, serious eyes drinking in my nude body. And suddenly self-consciousness pokes through my orgasmic cloud of pleasure at the inspection. "What do you see?" I need to hear his confirmation that he likes what's before him—rolls and all.

"A goddess meant to be worshipped."

Embarrassed at the divine comparison, I shake my head. "You don't have to exaggerate." Though, I appreciate the compliment. It's better than what he could've said.

"I'm not prone to hyperbole." He nips at my ear causing me to yelp in shock, hand batting playfully at his arm.

"You do know the way to a librarian's heart using a word like that." We both pause, realizing what I implied. Hearts. Love. He's probably not ready for such a serious confession even with all his talk of possession and being his. Those are just words—sex talk meant to hype my desire.

But Finn's gaze softens before he kisses me softly. "As long as I'm on the right track..."

Okay... Maybe we're not so far off from heartfelt declarations, after all.

"If you're ready, we can keep going. Or we can stop. It's up to you." His constant concern adds to the growing list of reasons I'm starting to fall for this man. Respectful and kind with a penchant for filthy talk, how could I not?

"Keep going. I want all of you."

Passion darkens his expression, and his thumb grazes my bottom lip. "And you'll have me. Every fucking inch." My breath stutters at the growled promise before his head lowers to my breasts, tongue flicking the distended buds. Trapping him against my chest with desperate hands, I urge him to take more, arching my back as an enticing offer, and he takes the bait, sucking hard on the sensitive tip.

"This what you want, baby? Me nursing at your tits while I fuck you?"

"God, yes..."

His erection grinds against my leg before he nestles it within my folds. The mushroom head stretching my untried flesh. Maybe I should've used all those toys Ella and Saoirse got me as gag gifts. *That might have been smart.* Then I could have avoided the slight burning sensation as he gingerly shifts forward.

"Fuck, Abby. You're so tight. You doing alright? Need me to take it slower?" Sweat drips down his temple at how controlled his movements are, the toll of his efforts obvious.

"No, I don't think drawing this part out will change the facts." I struggle to string together a cohesive thought. "Don't stop. Eventually, it'll get better." *Please, let me be right.*

He mumbles under his breath. "If I have any say, it will." Determination sets in on his face as a hand returns to my clit, building my pleasure again as a distraction from his thick cock moving ahead. The suction on my breast increases while he kneads my clit in rough succession. And it pays off as my body relaxes, loosening its grip and allowing Finn to slide deep.

A long exhale wafts over my cheeks at the blazing sensation before he draws back to plunge to the hilt again. The powerful rhythm slams me against the fluffy blankets and pillows cocooning us, and my mouth opens on a silent cry, eyes closing at the overload of emotions and physical contact.

This is how a man savagely claims his woman. It's in all the books I read. And now I have firsthand knowledge of how it feels to be full of lust, love, and his hard cock.

Another climax shatters my composure as the coarse fingering of my clit combines with the searing thrust of his hips to become an explosion of sparks.

"Finn!" His name flies from my lips in a whimper of fear—needing his reassurance, his grounding presence to anchor me to this moment.

"Don't worry, Abby-mine. I'm here; I've got you." He grunts the words out before his own body shudders in pleasure, a roar of release gushing between my thighs. Collapsing to the side, a strong arm wraps around my waist, tugging me close. "In a second, I'll grab a warm, clean cloth to clean us up."

"But you need a moment to recover?" I joke raggedly, smoothing a hand over the black ink covering his muscles. "Same."

Finn laps at my shoulder where his head nuzzles the exposed skin before kissing the spot. "Damn, you're too sweet. My cock's still regaining strength after fucking you, yet I can't get enough."

"You won't hear me complaining. I literally have decades to make up for." And if he's willing, I'm up for the challenge.

"A woman after my own heart." Finn chuckles and laces his fingers with mine. "We'll have a hell of a time making up for lost time."

You can bet on it.

CHAPTER NINE

FINN

A man like me has no right to be so happy, yet here I am fucking bursting with contentment and joy because I got the girl. *Damn, my girl.* We have filled the past week with conversations—serious and light-hearted—and fun outings. Not to mention the sex.

So. Much. Fucking.

But instead of spurring a waning of interest, my need for Abby keeps rising higher and higher. I don't think I'll ever be able to satisfy the well of need living inside me.

"And that's the last of the finishing touches. What do you think?" Abby agreed to let me draw another design on her other wrist this afternoon. This time I decided on a thicker, more intricate wristband suited for a Norse goddess—strong and beautiful, just like her.

"You've outdone yourself." She traces the outer edges, careful not to smudge the ink. "Now, I kind of wish I had a matching one for my other wrist."

"Next time," I promise, already imagining unique designs. Hell, I have a notebook chock full of Abby; ideas are never from mind when it comes to her. She's become my muse.

"I'll hold you to that." She smiles and leans forward to peck my cheek in a soft kiss. The ease of which astounds me. A week ago, I was getting her off without a hint of touching due to her hesitancy, and now? She fucking kissed me in public. My girl's brave and grown in confidence; something I love and take pride in helping her accomplish.

"Looks like you took the bet, after all." A snide voice breaks the intimate moment, and my blood freezes at the familiar arrival. Fucking Michael. What's he doing here?

I specifically check the books to make sure he's never around when Abby is, so she doesn't have to deal with his bullshit. Especially after she disclosed more about their brief relationship.

"What's he talking about?" Abby asks, her gaze darting between us.

"Didn't he tell you? I bet Finn that you wouldn't let him touch you. Guess I was wrong, huh?" His arrogant swagger pisses me off—not to mention the distress he's causing my girl.

"That's not true. I mean it is, but I didn't—"

She jerks her arm away from me and struggles out of the leather chair. "All of this was based on a bet?" Hurt clouds her features as my heart sinks to my gut at seeing her pain. "It was all a lie? God, Finn. We..." The words stutter to a halt, but their meaning is clear. We made love. She gave her virginity to me, and I betrayed her. *Except I didn't.*

"No, what we have is very real. Let me explain—"

A sharp hand raises to stop me. "Not now. Not like this." She motions to the small crowd of onlookers, staring curiously at the minor altercation. "We can talk later after I've had a moment to process through this."

Grabbing her purse, Abby tries to leave, but Michael blocks her way. "Come on now. Don't be mad. You should thank me for pushing Finn to take you on; we both know you needed help."

That's it.

Fury rages in my body, and my fist clenches before slamming into the bastard's face. Normally, I don't make a habit of assaulting customers, but Michael's pushed too far by insulting Abby.

"Finn!"

"What the fuck, man!"

Multiple exclamations of reprimand bombard me, but I don't care. He got what's been coming to him for weeks now. Abby grabs my stinging hand and gently prods the knuckles. "Are you alright? What were you thinking?"

"No one speaks to you like that," I growl.

"So, you were defending my honor?" She rolls her eyes, a huff of exasperation hitting the back of my hand. Satisfied with what she sees, Abby lets me go. "It doesn't look like you're too badly injured, and don't think I've forgotten this whole 'bet' debacle. I'll let you clean up this mess."

Sidestepping a whining Michael, she leaves, and I focus on controlling the damage I created. There will be plenty of time to grovel and beg for forgiveness from her later.

"You're going to pay for that; someone call the cops!" Michael shouts, gesturing wildly.

"There's no need to bring in the police, Mike. Just relax." Kyle tries calming him down. "You came in here with guns blazing and asking for trouble."

"Seriously? You're siding with him?"

"He's my boss, and on the right side of things here, though his choice of retaliation is questionable." Yeah, probably shouldn't have decked him, but I don't feel too badly about it. It was worth it to hear the crunch of his nose under my fist.

"I'll comp the rest of your tattoo." The grating concession slices down my throat. "But after that, you're not welcome here." I shoot Kyle an apologetic look, but he shrugs, knowing it's for the best.

Now, to figure out how to explain this clusterfuck to Abby without losing her forever.

CHAPTER TEN

ABIGAIL

A bet.

The only reason Finn pursued me.

The notion stings, though I don't find it as easy to believe as I did earlier. Or even if I'd found out a week ago. While our relationship might've started on false pretenses, I can't pretend that everything else hasn't felt genuine.

Finn has been nothing but caring and sweet—much more than I would've expected based on his rough looks. But as I like to warn library patrons: never judge a book by its cover. And this is exactly why. He'd upended all of my preconceived ideas about what a tatted and bearded man would be like, and despite the comparisons in looks, he's no Jax Teller from Sons of Anarchy.

Perhaps there's a reasonable explanation for everything. It's not like Michael is a reliable source. Even with the knowledge of this bet, I trust Finn infinitely more. I may even love him as crazy as it sounds.

Then what are you doing sitting here?

Grabbing my coat, I zip it up before pausing. "This is nuts," I say aloud to my empty living room. This isn't a movie; I can't just drive to Finn's house and profess my love for him. Can I?

Pulling out my phone, I pace the room while I send a video message to Ella and Saoirse, explaining the situation. "Am I crazy? Should I wait to hear his side of the story?"

Immediately, Ella replies with a slight scream as Gavin laughs in the background. "Do it! Oh my gosh, it'll be so romantic. You've always lived vicariously through books; now you can have your own fairytale ending!" Saoirse seconds the verdict with a block of thumbs up emojis. I should have guessed they'd be on board.

"Okay, I guess I'm doing this. Wish me luck." I end the message and scurry out to my car. The only thing that would make tonight perfect is if it started snowing. *And if it was still Christmas.* But I'll take love in January over none at all.

The streets lie deserted, though my route gets stalled at every red light. Finally, I park in Finn's driveway and wait for him to get home from the tattoo parlor. A lone porch light provides a bit of brightness to the otherwise dark night, and I settle on the top step leading to the front door. Rubbing gloved hands together, it'd be smarter to wait in my car instead of the cold weather, but how romantic is it to sit in your vehicle?

I want Finn to see me front and center when he arrives. If I were really bold, I'd run into his arms like the movies, but I'll skip that tradition. Booted feet stomp the concrete in more warming efforts, and I check the time. He should get home soon; we initially made plans tonight because his last client appointment wouldn't run super late.

What if he got arrested? The intrusive thought pushes forward. What if Michael pressed charges? It wouldn't be above him to do such a thing.

Before I can spiral down that rabbit hole, though, headlights flash and blind me for a second. The loud engine gets cut, and Finn jumps out of the car as I rise to my feet.

"Abby? What are you doing here? Are you okay?"

His concern kindles a fire in my belly that heats me from the inside out. No way this man agreed to some stupid bet to hurt me. He cares too much.

"I'm fine. I just needed to see you." Meeting him in the middle of the lawn, I wring my hands, sudden nerves tangling my tongue. "I've thought about what happened today, and while I still want to hear your story, it doesn't affect the way I feel about you. Unless, of course, this really was all a hoax..." I kind of laugh hysterically but try to rein it in. "But I don't think it was or is. You wouldn't hurt me intentionally; I truly believe that. You're the only man I've ever felt comfortable around, and that counts for a lot in my book."

Finn moves closer, arms circling my waist. "You have no idea how much that means to me, baby. Michael offered the bet weeks ago, but I turned him down because I don't play silly games. Especially not with the woman I'm falling in love with."

My eyes widen in surprise at the declaration. *Well, damn.* He beat me to it. "Noble of you. And I'm falling for you, too. We're kind of the fast and furious, aren't we?" I joke. The speed with which we jumped into bed to in love is lightning quick but perfect in my eyes.

"What can we say? We know what we want."

"You know what else I want?" One of his eyebrows raises in question. "For you to take me out of this cold and make love to me."

A playful grin peeks out of his bearded face before he tugs me towards the front door. "Whatever my lady commands."

EPILOGUE ONE

FINN

ONE YEAR LATER

"Are you sure you want to do this? It's unnecessary." Abby's worried voice sounds above the buzzing of the tattoo machine as Kyle continues working on my latest addition.

"Positive, baby. I want your permanent mark on me." Scrolling script that reads 'Abby-mine' is going across my heart in an uncharacteristically sentimental gesture. But what can I say? My woman made me soft, and I'm not mad about it.

She bites her bottom lip, eyes following the motions of Kyle's hand. Squeezing the sweaty hand in mine for comfort, I try again to allay her fears. "Don't worry; you're not losing me. This is forever." I stroke the diamond ring on her finger as a reminder.

Three months after her birthday, I proposed to Abby, and we eloped the next month. Our entire relationship has run fast and hot, so we didn't see the wisdom in planning an elaborate wedding months in advance. Now, Abby's officially mine—tied to me for good.

"I know..." A soft smile loosens some of the tension on her face as she returns the hard squeeze. "I just like to worry."

"Why don't you focus that energy on next month's party?" In honor of her best friend's pregnancy, she'd agreed to host a baby shower at our place. Something I hoped we'd be having for ourselves soon. For all our speed, everyone expected us to get pregnant right away, but we both agreed it'd be nice to relax with just the two of us for the time being.

Though the look in my girl's eyes when talking about the baby stuff lets me know that time is ending. And hell, if I won't enjoy trying to knock her up.

"You're right. There's a lot to prepare." She starts rattling off a list of things to do, and I sink back into my seat—glad I succeeded in getting her mind off the tattoo. Her sweet voice calms me, and my hand itches to draw her. Again. By now, I've worn out numerous pencils and filled copious notebooks of her—clothed and nude.

But it's never enough. Never will be because I adore my Abby-mine.

She's my heart. My life.

EPILOGUE TWO

ABIGAIL
TEN YEARS LATER

Screaming children clamber around the backyard while the men tend to the grill. Ella, Saoirse, and I are enjoying our minor break from the chaos by sipping ice cold margaritas by the pool at Ella and Gavin's house.

"Can you believe this is our life? Adorable kids, though they can be little gremlins and hot fucking husbands. Like damn. The Tees & Jeans Club did good." Saoirse raises her glass in salute. And I couldn't agree more.

At times, the road was bumpy, but we all made it—intact and in love.

"We sure did." Ella shields her eyes as she watches Gavin flip a couple of burger patties. "And we didn't have to change who we were to accomplish it. Our promise from all those years ago remains true."

"Well, we changed a little," I amend, thinking back to when the idea of a man touching me sent anxiety raging through my body. *So glad I got past that.* My hungry eyes travel over Finn—shirtless and in swim shorts, all of his tattoos on display.

"But that was naturally evolving as we grew up. We never compromised our values, though."

"True." Even though I came close when I dated Michael, I can't regret that decision too much since it led me to my husband. Otherwise, I'm not sure Finn and I ever would have met, and that would have been devastating.

He's the kind of man I always wished for and read about but never really expected to find in real life. But he proved me wrong and exceeded those expectations. Passionate and protective, I've never had a moment's doubt about his love for me.

As if aware we're talking about them, all three guys glance over at us before Finn walks over with a bottle of water. "Remember to drink this, baby. The way you're downing the tequila, I don't want you to get a headache."

"I'll be fine, but thank you." Sitting up from the lounge chair, I tilt my head to receive a quick kiss from him. *Yum.*

"You guys are too cute even if you make the oddest looking couple."

I laugh because it's true. Everyone always stares at the tatted hulk beside me in my cardigans and glasses. But who cares?

Opposites attract, right?

And we form one combustible combination of love and desire that I wouldn't trade for anything in the world.

Don't miss the Lumberjacks of High Ridge!

These lumberjacks weren't looking for love, but high on the mountain, it's about to find them when their curvy soulmates arrive!

Kept by the Beast (Book #1)

All Poppy wanted was a relaxing trip to the cute mountain town of High Ridge. She didn't plan on getting stranded with no one to call for help. What's a shy, curvy girl to do?

Asa is known as the town's Beast. Large and foreboding, women run in fear and revulsion. But when this mountain man happens upon a curvy damsel in distress, could she be the one woman to accept him for who he is?

Two virgins stranded in a cabin...Things are heating up on the mountain when a curvy girl meets this beastly lumberjack in a steamy story of insta-love!

THANKS FOR READING & DON'T FORGET TO RATE/ REVIEW!

Please consider leaving a rating/review on Amazon, Goodreads, Instagram, TikTok, and/or any other sites you review on.

Ratings & reviews are the #1 way to support an indie author like me.

They don't have to be long or even positive (though I hope you enjoyed this book!). All the algorithms care about are QUANTITY.

The more reviews, the more my books are shown to other potential readers!

And they serve as guides to readers on whether or not to take a chance on an indie author.

I appreciate your support!

XO, Hallie

ABOUT THE AUTHOR

Hallie prefers steamy, insta-love stories where curvy girls are claimed by filthy-talking heroes. And when she ran out of reading material, she decided to write her own stories. If you want a quick, hot read, she's your girl!

Lightning Source UK Ltd.
Milton Keynes UK
UKHW012214130223
416920UK00006B/1080